To the artists and makers who
use their creativity, ingenuity,
and wild imaginations to conjure
up the magical delight of
Brazilian Carnival every year.
Thank you for your spark.

All rights reserved. Published in the United States by Random House Studio,
an imprint of Random House Children's Books,
a division of Penguin Random House LLC, New York.

Random House Studio with colophon is a registered trademark of Penguin Random House LLC.

Visit us on the Web! rhcbooks.com

Educators and librarians, for a variety of teaching tools, visit us at RHTeachersLibrarians.com

Library of Congress Cataloging-in-Publication Data is available upon request.
ISBN 978-0-593-38009-3 (trade) — ISBN 978-0-593-38010-9 (lib. bdg.) — ISBN 978-0-593-38011-6 (ebook)

The artist used digital tools to create the illustrations for this book.
The text of this book is set in 23-point Tomarik.
Interior design by Rachael Cole

MANUFACTURED IN CHINA
10 9 8 7 6 5 4 3 2 1
First Edition

THE SPARK IN YOU

ANDREA PIPPINS

RANDOM HOUSE STUDIO  NEW YORK

There's a spark in you,
and whenever you have an idea

BRASIL

CARNAVAL

it dances in your smile,

through your hands,

and in your feet.

Your spark is with you
wherever you go,

shimmering when you discover something new.

It is full of wonderful
color,

PASTEL e
COXINHA

ACARAJÉ

FRUTA:
AÇAÍ, MANGA,
ABACAXI

SORVETE

and it zings and pops
with delight.

Even when everything feels busy and

LOUD,

it is there, glowing as quiet comfort in your heart.

Your spark is big and powerful
like a festive explosion,

It is so warm and bright that everyone feels it, too,

that beautiful spark
BEAMING
inside of you.

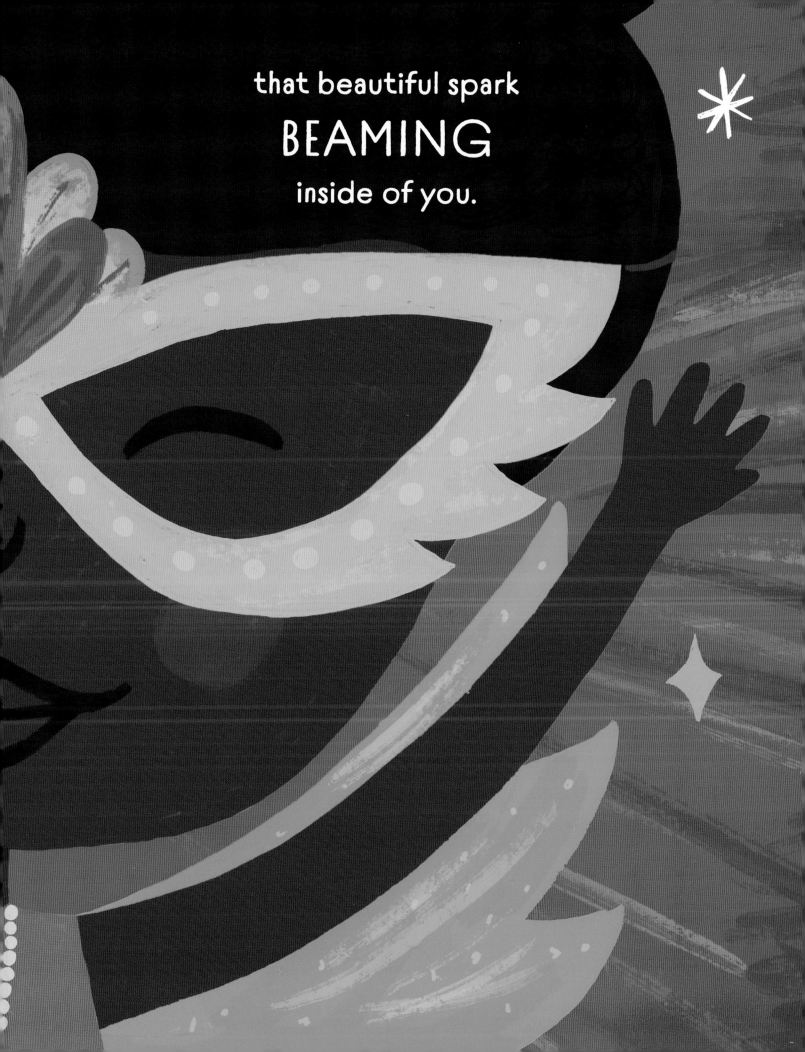

make your own
FANCY MASK

Here's what you'll need:

CONSTRUCTION PAPER

SCISSORS

PAINT

GLUE

SEQUINS

BUTTONS

RIBBON

STRING

STICK

ELASTIC BAND

DRAWING TOOL

feathers

Here's what to do:

1

Start by drawing your mask on the paper.

2

Cut out the mask and the eye holes.

3

With the stick or a pencil point, make holes for your string, ribbon, or elastic band.

4

To measure your string, ribbon, or elastic band, cut it to the width of your head from ear to ear (from the back of your head). Leave a little extra to tie. An elastic band can be slightly shorter because it stretches.

5

Add color to your mask, such as with paint, crayons, or markers.

6

Add your decorative elements. Avoid covering the holes.

7

Pull the string, ribbon, or elastic band through the holes. Tie a knot to hold it in place.

Another option: Glue your stick to the back of the mask. Then you will use the stick to hold the mask up to your face.